What is Indiana Jones doing in Princeton in February 1916?

Indy shifts gears fast when car trouble plunges him into a mystery! German spies may be at work, but Indy's not on the track alone. His girlfriend, Nancy, is a super sleuth. She's smart, pretty, and . . . totally fearless.

Ride along with the two of them, and keep your eyes open for reckless drivers!

Catch the whole story of Young Indy's travels on the amazing fact-and-fiction television series *The Young Indiana Jones Chronicles!*

THE YOUNG INDIANA JONES CHRONICLES

(novels based on the television series)

TV-1. The Mummy's Curse

TV-2. Field of Death

TV-3. Safari Sleuth

TV-4. The Secret Peace

TV-5. Trek of Doom

TV-6. Revolution!

TV-7. Race to Danger

TV-8. Prisoner of War

YOUNG INDIANA JONES BOOKS

(original novels)

Young Indiana Jones and the . . .

1. Plantation Treasure

2. Tomb of Terror

3. Circle of Death

4. Secret City

5. Princess of Peril

6. Gypsy Revenge

7. Ghostly Riders

8. Curse of the Ruby Cross

Race to Danger

Adapted by Stephanie Calmenson

Based on the teleplay "Princeton, February 1916"
by Matthew Jacobs

Directed by Joe Johnston

Story by George Lucas

With photographs from the television show

Random House   New York

This is a work of fiction. While Young Indiana Jones is portrayed as taking part in historical events and meeting real figures from history, many of the characters in the story as well as the situations and scenes have been invented. In addition, where real historical figures and events are described, in some cases the chronology and historical facts have been altered for dramatic effect.

Photo credits: Cover and interior photographs by Jaromir Komarek, © 1993 by Lucasfilm Ltd. (LFL). Map by Jan Lebeyka.

Library of Congress Cataloging-in-Publication Data:
Calmenson, Stephanie.
   Race to danger / adapted by Stephanie Calmenson ; story by George Lucas ; directed by Joe Johnston.
     p. cm. — (The Young Indiana Jones Chronicles ; TV-7)
   "Based on the teleplay 'Princeton, February 1916' by Matthew Jacobs . . . with photographs from the television show."
   Summary: Young Indiana Jones and his girlfriend, daughter of Tom Swift creator Edward Stratemeyer, are visiting the laboratories of Thomas A. Edison when top secret plans for an electric car are stolen.
   ISBN 0-679-84388-4 (pbk.)
   [1. Adventure and adventurers—Fiction. 2. Edison, Thomas A. (Thomas Alva), 1847–1931—Fiction.] I. Lucas, George. II. Johnston, Joe. III. Jacobs, Matthew. IV. Title. V. Series.
PZ7.C136Rac 1993   [Fic]—dc20   92-56396

Race to Danger

INDY'S TERRITORY IN "PRINCETON, FEBRUARY 1916"

NEW YORK

NEW JERSEY

West Orange

Bayonne

New York City

Princeton

★ Trenton

PENNSYLVANIA

Atlantic Ocean

Philadelphia

DELAWARE

N
W—E
S

0   50 Miles

Chapter 1

Everyone in town was talking about the weather. Was it a winter thaw or an amazingly early spring? The mercury had risen so high that *The Princeton Press* had been running front-page stories for three days in a row. Scientists from Princeton University were speculating about possible causes.

People who hardly ever noticed the weather

were talking about it. Even Young Indiana Jones's father had asked Indy if it wasn't unusually warm for February. And Professor Jones was so wrapped up in his studies that he usually didn't know what season it was.

But Indiana Jones wasn't wondering about the weather. He was *enjoying* it. For one thing, Mr. Harper, who owned the ice cream parlor where Indy worked as a soda jerk, had put him on afternoons after school. Indy usually worked at Harper's Ice Cream Parlor only on Saturdays. But the warm weather seemed to make folks thirsty for a lemon phosphate or a root beer float. Mr. Harper was humming his favorite song, "In the Good Old Summertime," and smiling while the cash register jingled.

Indy was glad to have a chance to earn some extra money, even if it meant missing the tryouts for the baseball team. The Valentine Dance was just days away. It was going to cost a small fortune by Indy's standards. He had already paid for the tickets, but he wanted to buy a corsage for his girlfriend, Nancy Stratemeyer. And right now Indy was sitting up in the bleachers at his high school waiting for her.

He was still wearing his clothes from gym class. The sun warmed his fingers as he quickly turned the pages of the book he was reading. It was just one of the many books Nancy's dad, Edward Stratemeyer, had written. It was called *Tom Swift and His Amazing Electric Car.*

Tom Swift, the young inventor, was taking his sleek electric car around the track as fast as it could go in a death-defying race. Mary Nestor, his girlfriend, was by his side.

Indy imagined he could hear the roar of the crowd as they cheered Tom Swift on. He began reading more quickly. His eyes darted back and forth across the page.

By the time Tom Swift won the race, Indy was almost out of breath himself.

"Well, are we going to try some more races?" asked Mary hopefully.

"Mary," said Tom, "you've got brains, luck,

and dollops of pluck. But I don't believe I'll go in for any more races right away. I've been wanting to . . ."

Suddenly the book was whisked out of Indy's hands.

"My gosh, Indy! If my father knew you spent all your time reading his books, what would he think of you?" said Nancy.

"Come on, Nancy. They're great!" said Indy.

"Hey, guess what?" said Nancy. "Mom is taking me this afternoon to get a dress for the Valentine Dance. I'm so excited!"

"Butch is going to go green with envy when he hears I'm taking your father's car to the prom," said Indy.

Indy and Nancy walked as far as the gym together. Then Nancy headed for home, and Indy went toward the entrance to the gymnasium to change.

He saw Butch's Model T parked outside.

"Anybody want to go for a quick spin before the tryouts?" called Butch.

Butch liked acting like a big shot. He could

usually get away with it. First, he had just been named the captain of the baseball team by Coach Patterson. Second, he drove his father's Model T as though it was his very own.

A group of guys piled into Butch's car. Clifford dashed up front to turn the crank and start the motor.

"Too bad you guys are going to have to get to the prom with shoe leather," said Butch, grinning.

"Maybe some of us won't have to, Butch," said Indy. "I'm driving a car to the prom that's better than that turkey Model T."

"Oh, yeah? Like what?" asked Butch.

"Like a Bugatti," said Indy.

Everyone turned at once as if the word were magic.

"A Bugatti!" said Butch.

There wasn't a sharper car in town than Edward Stratemeyer's Bugatti. It had a front end that was about a mile long, and whitewall tires with hubcaps as shiny as mirrors. It had two great big headlights. And it was in mint condition. There wasn't a scratch on it.

"That's right. Nancy's father's letting me take his car," said Indy.

"You can't kid me, buddy. Her dad won't let you drive that car!" said Butch.

"Just you wait and see," said Indy.

Indy smiled and walked into the gym feeling like a million dollars. He went into the locker room and quickly changed his clothes. He didn't want to be late getting to work.

The ice cream parlor was jam-packed, and Mr. Harper was humming away. He checked his gold pocket watch and nodded approvingly as Indy took his place behind the marble counter.

Indy started scooping out ice cream as if it were going out of style. Once in while he missed a dish and cooled his toes with a scoop of strawberry or chocolate.

Working as a soda jerk was not the most exciting thing Indy had ever done. In fact, he had been on adventures all over the world. Or just about.

That is because Indy's father was a professor of medieval literature at Princeton University. Thanks to his lecture tours, Indy had seen the ancient pyramids of Egypt and been in the teeming cities of China and India.

Professor Jones had ideas about money that were medieval too. No one had given the Knights of the Round Table an allowance! It was up to Indy to earn his own spending money.

"One double fudge sundae, please," said sixteen-year-old Rosie in her bubbly cheerleader voice. "And don't forget to put a cherry on top, Indy!"

"One double fudge sundae with a cherry coming right up," said Indy.

Indy was fixing up Rosie's sundae when Butch walked in. He put his arm around Rosie's shoulders and squeezed till she squealed.

Then he turned to Indy. "You never made it to the baseball tryouts today. Why not, soda *jerk*?" he said.

"Some of us have to work for our allowance, Butch," replied Indy. He skillfully fished a cherry out of the jar for Rosie's sundae.

"Oh, my poor heart bleeds!" said Butch, clutching his chest.

"Anyway, it's okay. I told Mr. Patterson I'll

be there once regular practice starts," said Indy.

"Don't bother. Clifford here proved to be a fine fielder. Didn't you, Clifford?" said Butch.

Butch moved down two stools to where Clifford was sitting. He gave Clifford a bear hug. It turned his face almost as red as his hair. Clifford was so skinny that it didn't take much to knock the wind out of him.

"Whoa! Whatever you say, Butch," said Clifford, when he was able to breathe again.

"You did just fine, Clifford, my man. That is, when you were running in the right direction!" Butch laughed.

Clifford laughed too. He didn't exactly get the joke. But if Butch was laughing, something had to be funny.

"So, Butch, what will you have? The same as Rosie? Or an ice cream soda? Or maybe a root beer float?" asked Indy.

"I'd drink sewer water before I let anything you've touched pass my lips," said Butch.

Indy bit back the answer he was dying to

make. The last thing he wanted to do was lose his job. What he felt like saying would lead to a fistfight for sure.

No, Indy would answer Butch soon enough. And without words. He just had to wait a few more days until the dance.

"Come over here and sit with me, Butch," said Rosie. She flashed him a smile as she led him to a table.

Indy was not the least bit sorry to see Butch go. He moved to the end of the counter to talk to Nancy. Her pretty face, framed by her long, dark hair, was buried in a copy of *Tom Swift and His Great Oil Gusher*.

"That must be a brand-new one. Is it any good?" asked Indy.

"The book you were reading was better. I told Dad he should change the ending of this one," said Nancy quietly.

"You look down in the dumps, Nance. What's the matter? Couldn't you find a dress you liked?" asked Indy.

"The first dress I tried on was perfect. That's

not the problem. I don't want to tell you what's bothering me. You will be devastated," said Nancy.

"No, I won't. Go ahead and tell me," said Indy.

Nancy sighed. Then she put down her book and looked Indy straight in the eyes. "We're not going to be able to take Dad's car to the dance," she said all in one breath.

"*What!*" exclaimed Indy. He hated to admit it, but Nancy was right. He was devastated.

Indy usually wasn't hung up on luxuries. But this Bugatti—well, it was in a class by itself. And it would put Butch in his place in no time flat.

"The car wouldn't start this morning," explained Nancy. "Dad's got to take it to New York to get it fixed. It will take weeks."

"But the dance is this Saturday!" cried Indy.

"I know, I know. I told him," said Nancy.

"Your dad promised. I told everyone I'm driving you to the dance in his Bugatti," said Indy. "When Butch heard I was driving that car, he turned green with envy. This is disastrous!"

For weeks, Indy had been picturing himself driving Nancy to the dance in that car.

"There's nothing we can do, Indy," said Nancy. "It's not Dad's fault that the car won't start. It's not as if he changed his mind."

"I know," said Indy. "It's just such a let-down. This means we'll have to double-date with Clifford! His dad is going to let him use his truck."

Clifford heard his name. He looked up, grinned, and waved.

"Oh, no, not that!" said Nancy. "At least let's go with Ricky."

Just then Ricky walked in the door. Really, he walked right *into* the door. He was not looking where he was going. He was looking at the "knockout twins," who had just walked out of the ice cream parlor. He was trying to figure out which one was Kathy and which one was Karen. That's when he smashed facefirst into the glass door. Once again the girls had earned their nickname.

Ricky staggered inside, rubbing his battered nose.

"Go with Ricky?" said Indy, shaking his head. "I don't think so."

Chapter 2

When Indy's work shift was over, he walked Nancy home. He wanted to try to talk to Mr. Stratemeyer. He thought he knew a way to get the car fixed before the dance on Saturday.

A childhood friend of his dad's, Jack Williams, had opened a service station at the edge of town a long time ago. It was called Williams Brothers' Garage. Jack Williams had died a few years back. But his brother Bert kept the business running. Jack's daughter, Jewel, worked at the garage too. And not as a bookkeeper. She had become a crackerjack mechanic. Her father would have been proud of her.

Most people thought it was pretty strange for a sixteen-year-old girl to be a mechanic. But Jewel was an only child. Her mother had died when she was ten years old. Jewel and her dad had been very close. She had spent a lot of time with him at the garage when she was growing up. He taught her everything there was to know about cars. If Jewel couldn't fix the Bugatti, Indy didn't know who could!

Nancy opened the white gate that led up to her house.

"Daddy's probably working. But I don't think he'll mind if we interrupt him," she said.

She knocked lightly on the door of her father's study. Mr. Stratemeyer was so busy typing the manuscript for his latest book that he did not hear her.

Indy studied the walls he had seen so many times before. Hanging over the bookcase was the cover of Mr. Stratemeyer's very first Tom Swift mystery, *Tom Swift and His Motorcycle*. Next to the cover was a picture of Tom Swift's real-life inspiration, inventor Glenn Curtiss, standing beside his real-life motorbike.

Over the desk, which was cluttered with books and papers, were drawings of the Bobbsey Twins, the Moving Picture Girls, and other characters Nancy's dad had created.

Mr. Stratemeyer was an amazing writing machine! He wrote hundreds of stories, all under different names. He used the name Victor Appleton when he wrote the Tom Swift stories. Laura Lee Hope was the name he used for the Bobbsey Twins and the Moving Picture Girls. And he was Roy Rockwood, Jack Lancer, Margaret Penrose, Captain Quincey Adams, and a host of other "people" as well.

But to his family he was just one person— hardworking, straight-laced, and dependable Dad. And Nancy knew she could depend on him to be miles away, wherever his heroes were taking him.

"Ahem!" said Nancy, loudly enough for her father to hear.

"Oh, hello, Nance. Hello, Indy," said Mr. Stratemeyer, looking up over his wire-rimmed spectacles.

Edward Stratemeyer looked more like a banker than a writer. He wore a dark gray suit, starched white shirt, and perfectly knotted maroon tie.

Nancy once told Indy how her father got started writing. He had always loved to read. He read as many dime-store novels as he could get his hands on. But he had dropped out of school after the eighth grade. So at the age of twenty-seven, the best job he could get was working in his brother's tobacco store.

On a particularly slow afternoon, Edward Stratemeyer tore some brown wrapping paper from a roll. Then he took a pen and began to write a story. It was called "Victor Horton's Idea." He sent it in on that very same brown wrapping paper to a boys' magazine called *Golden Days*. The magazine bought the story for seventy-five dollars, which was six times as much as he made in a week at the tobacco store. Edward Stratemeyer was suddenly a working writer.

"Good afternoon, sir," said Indy. "How's the new Tom Swift story coming?"

"It's giving me some trouble, Indy. I've got Tom stuck in an Incan tomb, surrounded by rocket rangers, and his stun gun doesn't work. The villain is flooding the tomb, and I don't know how to get Tom out," said Nancy's father.

"Hmm. Have you read Hiram Bingham's account of the discovery of the ruins of Machu Picchu?" asked Indy.

"No, I haven't," said Mr. Stratemeyer.

"He discovered this amazing Inca city about five years ago. I've been reading about his discoveries in *National Geographic* magazine," continued Indy.

"Tell me about it," said Mr. Stratemeyer, picking up a pencil to take notes.

"Well, the Incas were very skilled stonemasons. Bingham thinks there might be a complex maze of underground tunnels under Machu Picchu. But he doesn't want to open them up because he's afraid the whole thing will collapse. I bet if you got Tom into the tunnels, he could give the villains the slip, or corner them."

"Thank you, Indy. I'll give that some thought," said Mr. Stratemeyer.

By this time, Nancy was jabbing Indy in the ribs with her elbow.

"The car. Talk to Dad about the car," she whispered.

"Oh, right. Um, er, Mr. Stratemeyer, sir. About your car . . ." stammered Indy.

"Yes, I'm sorry about that," said Mr. Stratemeyer.

"I was thinking," said Indy, "about someone I know who just might be able to fix it. Her name's Jewel Williams. She's over at Williams Brothers' Garage at the edge of town. If anyone around here could do it, she could."

"I don't know," said Mr. Stratemeyer. "I've heard this Jewel Williams is pretty good. But I don't know that I want some sixteen-year-old girl fiddling with my Bugatti."

"Oh, really? And how about if she was a sixteen-year-old *boy*?" asked Nancy.

"No, no. That's not it at all," said Mr. Stratemeyer. "That Bugatti is a beautiful piece of machinery. The people in New York work on those cars all the time."

"Sir, I know I can get it fixed. I promise you!" said Indy.

"Please, Father, we'll be careful with it," pleaded Nancy.

"Oh, all right," said Mr. Stratemeyer. "But be *very* careful, understand?"

"Gee whiz, Mr. Stratemeyer, you're swell!" cried Indy.

Mr. Stratemeyer had already turned back to his typewriter.

"Get ready, Tom," he said to a blank piece of paper. "You're about to go down into the tunnels of Machu Picchu."

When they were out of the study, Nancy said to Indy, "Father always asks you about Tom Swift. He never asks me."

It bothered Nancy that her father refused to recognize her flair for adventure and mystery.

"He asks you about the Bobbsey Twins," said Indy.

"Big deal. I could have worked out that Inca thing, easy peasy," said Nancy.

"Easy peasy?" said Indy.

"I wouldn't talk if I were you, Mr. Gee Whiz, That's Swell!" replied Nancy.

"I guess we're even," said Indy. "Now let's get that car to the garage!"

Chapter 3

Indy hitched the shiny Bugatti up to his horse. Nancy sat behind the steering wheel. With passersby cheering them on, they made it to Williams' Brothers Garage without a snag.

Indy and Nancy watched as Jewel expertly checked the Bugatti.

"So, can you fix it?" asked Indy hopefully.

Jewel was the same age as Nancy. Even with

her grease-stained overalls, she was worth a second look. She had a red bandanna tying back her black curly hair, green eyes, and a major crush on Indy.

Jewel thought Indy was the best-looking guy in Princeton. But that wasn't all. Indy was a real friend—someone she could count on. He always defended her whenever people joked about her being a mechanic. And sometimes the teasing could be cruel.

"Gosh, I wish I could fix it," said Jewel. "You know I'd do *anything* for you, Indy."

"You could start by telling us what the problem is," said Nancy, a little too impatiently.

"It's the generator," said Jewel. "And the only place to get a new one is in France. But you know what's going on there."

Indy had heard long discussions about the war that was raging in Europe. It had started when an assassin named Gavrilo Princip shot Archduke Franz Ferdinand of Austria-Hungary. How one murder could start a war involving so many different countries was still confusing to Indy. But he knew that the countries of France, Britain, and Russia called themselves the Allies. They were fighting Austria-Hungary and Germany, who called themselves the Central Powers. The United States was still neutral. But for how long?

Well, for now there was nothing Indy could do about this terrible war. And he had his own problem to solve. He had to get the Bugatti engine fixed. The future of the world might not depend on it. But getting to the dance on Saturday did.

"There must be someone around who knows how to fix this thing," said Indy.

"I doubt it. Unless you know a scientific genius," said Jewel. "I'm sorry I couldn't fix the car, Indy. If you need anything else, you know where to find me."

"Thanks, Jewel," said Indy.

Nancy slipped behind the steering wheel of the Bugatti just as Indy was getting on his horse.

Honk! Honk! Butch was driving past in his Model T and couldn't resist a chance to be nasty.

"Hey there, soda *jerk*! Are you going to ride your horse to the dance on Saturday?" he called.

"Or do you have a bicycle built for two in the next stall?"

"No way. You just wait till we get this car fixed up!" answered Indy. Butch's taunting was really getting under his skin.

When Butch was gone, Indy walked over to Nancy. "There's got to be a way to fix the Bugatti," he said. "There's just got to be!"

"Don't worry about it, Indy," said Nancy. "We'll just be like almost everyone else and walk to the prom."

"Everyone except Butch," said Indy.

"You're not going to the prom with Butch. You're going with me!" said Nancy.

"Yeah, I know," said Indy. "It's just that . . ."

"Forget about Butch! The only person you need to impress is me . . . and I'm impressed," said Nancy.

"I've just got to think of some way to get that car running," said Indy.

He walked over to his horse and climbed back on it. Luckily the horse knew the way. Indy's mind was on the Bugatti behind him—not the road in front of him.

He dropped Nancy and the Bugatti off at her house. Then he rode the horse back home.

His dad was having a dinner party. Indy could see that the party was already under way. The house was brightly lit. He could hear glasses clinking and voices raised in conversation.

Indy stabled the horse and poured out some oats. Then he slipped into the house, washed up, and went to the dining room. He stood at the door for a moment, just watching.

He counted ten guests. Most of them were from Princeton University. Princeton University, with its medieval style buildings draped with ivy, was the perfect setting for Professor Jones. The university dining hall even had stained-glass windows that told the story of the search for the Holy Grail, the cup which Christ had used at the Last Supper.

Fortunately, the dining room at home was much less formal. Indy looked around the table. All the seats were filled, except for one. That was for Indy.

In Indy's mind, there was still one more empty

place—the place opposite his father's. That was where his mother, Anna, would be. She had died four years ago. Indy could still see her face, with her blue eyes and soft smile, as clear as day.

"Junior, come sit down," said Professor Jones. "There's a seat here for you between me and Dr. Thompson. You remember Dr. Thompson, don't you?"

"Yes. Good evening, Dr. Thompson," said Indy. But the only thing on Indy's mind at that moment was why, oh, why, does my father insist on calling me Junior!

Indy hated being called Junior. His mother had called him Henry. That was the name he was given when he was born—Henry Jones, Jr. Some of his teachers called him Henry. But everyone else called him Indy or Indiana. Everyone, that is, but his father.

There was no changing his father's mind. Even when Indy became old and gray, Professor Jones would still be calling him Junior.

"Dr. Thompson used to teach at the university, Junior. These days he is working at Thomas

Edison's West Orange plant," explained Professor Jones. "So, John, what's it like working for big industry?"

"Since I left Princeton I'm discovering that research for Edison and academic research are two entirely different worlds. You see, Edison puts his ideas to work. Take the battery, for example. When I perfect the Edison battery, the age of the internal combustion engine will be over," said Dr. Thompson.

"How can you make a battery that will last long enough?" asked Professor Jones.

"The details of the plan are Edison's secret," replied Dr. Thompson. "But I can tell you that Henry Ford believes in that plan enough to pay for the research."

"Hmm. An electric Model T. With a battery like that, the oil companies would be put out of business," said Professor Jones thoughtfully.

"Did you ever read *Tom Swift and His Amazing Electric Car* by Edward Stratemeyer, Dr. Thompson?" asked Indy excitedly.

"Can't say that I did, Indy," said Dr. Thompson.

"It came out about five years ago," continued Indy.

"Junior, you're interrupting!" exclaimed Professor Jones.

"Sorry. It's just that Tom Swift invented a lithium and potassium-hydrate battery, and the car went a hundred miles an hour!" said Indy.

"Well, that's just one of Mr. Stratemeyer's fantasies, Indy," said Dr. Thompson. "Edison's battery is a reality. It's very exciting. Electric cars will be noiseless, and there will be no exhaust."

Indy was absorbing all the information he was hearing about electric cars. He was thinking how nice it would be to have a car without exhaust when he overheard Mrs. Thompson talking to the person next to her.

"My husband is a true scientific genius," Indy heard Mrs. Thompson say.

Scientific genius? The words echoed in his head. Then he remembered where he had heard them before. Jewel said it would take a scientific genius to get the Bugatti's generator fixed. Dr. Thompson could be just the man he was looking for.

Chapter 4

After dinner, Indy approached Dr. Thompson. Making sure his father was out of earshot, Indy told Dr. Thompson all about the dance and the Bugatti and the busted generator.

"Do you think you could reconstruct the generator for us?" asked Indy.

Dr. Thompson smiled. "Even my assistant, Mr. Dickinson, could do it," he said.

"Really?" asked Indy.

"Sure," said Dr. Thompson.

"Could I bring it over to the West Orange lab tomorrow?" asked Indy. He took a quick look over his shoulder to make sure his dad wasn't listening.

"Well, tomorrow is a busy day," said Dr. Thompson. "No, wait. On second thought, tomorrow would not be bad at all. Come by tomorrow."

"Gosh, thanks, Dr. Thompson!" cried Indy, a little too loudly. He was so happy, he forgot that his father might hear him.

Luckily, Professor Jones had just gone into the library. He had gotten into a disagreement with Dr. Shaw, an art historian. It was about a detail on the left portal of the cathedral at Chartres in France. He wanted to check his sources.

Meanwhile, Indy could hardly believe his good luck. Dr. Thompson was going to see about getting the Bugatti running. And Indy was going to see the Edison laboratory!

Indy slipped off to call Nancy. They made a

plan to meet at the train station early the next morning.

That night, Indy remembered how he had fought his tutor, Miss Seymour, when she wanted him to read about the great inventor. Indy was in Paris at the time, and had plans to meet a friend. Instead, he had to stay in his room with a pile of books.

Reading about Edison was not as much fun as exploring Paris. But it wasn't boring either. Indy tried to remember some of the things he had learned.

He knew that Edison was born in Ohio. He was the youngest child in the large family of Samuel and Nancy Edison.

When he was seven, Edison got scarlet fever. His illness left him nearly deaf.

Edison was not a very good student. He annoyed his teacher by playing tricks. He kept interrupting the class with his questions. And because he could not hear, it seemed he could not learn. In fact, his teacher once said that he might be retarded. When Edison's mother heard that, she took him right out of school. She taught him his lessons at home.

This "retarded" student then went on to become one of the greatest inventors of all time.

The thing Indy thought was so great about Edison was that he didn't invent things just to prove how smart he was. He invented and improved things to help people live better. His inventions were both practical and wonderful. Thanks to Edison there were the electric light, the phonograph, the telephone, the copying machine, and motion pictures.

Indy fell asleep dreaming that he was the star of a motion picture, driving around in his shiny Bugatti.

The next morning he got up and went to pick up Nancy and the generator. Luckily, there was no school.

"It was really nice of this Dr. Thompson to offer to help us out," said Nancy.

"It sure was!" said Indy.

At the station, they piled their bicycles and

the Bugatti generator onto the first train heading for West Orange, New Jersey.

The train chugged past a neat patchwork of fields and chicken farms. It was pretty, but it was a whole lot less exciting than where they were going.

The trip seemed to take forever. But finally they reached their destination.

"Can you believe this place!" said Indy as they rode their bikes up to the Edison plant gates.

The plant was an enormous complex of buildings. The main building was three stories high. The walls were draped with ivy, which framed the tall, arched windows.

Indy had read somewhere that Edison's library was inside the main building. There were two tiers of balconies with shelves holding thousands of technical books.

Edison had an enormous clock hanging on the wall over his desk. He said he kept it there to remind him that time was precious. If anyone knew that, Edison did. He did not like to waste even a second. It was said that he once worked on the phonograph for seventy-two hours *nonstop.*

Dr. Thompson had told Indy some of the things that went on inside the other buildings. For example, there was Edison's work connecting sound with moving pictures. And then there was his latest invention—the battery that would make gasoline-driven cars obsolete.

Indy and Nancy rode their bikes up to a security guard.

"Could you please tell us how to get to Dr. Thompson's lab?" Indy asked.

"Certainly. That would be the Chemistry Lab. It's over there," said the guard.

He pointed the way to a group of low sheds. The sheds were encircled by a racetrack. Suddenly a car careened around the track, leaving a cloud of dust in its wake.

"Wow! Look at that!" cried Indy.

"Over here, Indy! I'm over here!" called a voice.

When the dust cleared, Indy could see Dr. Thompson. He was standing just inside one of the open sheds right next to his baby—a shiny model electric car.

"Hi, Dr. Thompson. This is my friend Nancy Stratemeyer," said Indy.

"Hello, Nancy," said Dr. Thompson.

"And here's the generator!" said Indy.

"As I was telling Indy, someday generators will be obsolete," said Dr. Thompson. "We'll get Edison's electric battery perfected. Then we won't need generators to convert gasoline into energy. The power supply will be constant."

"Yes, Dr. Thompson. Indy was telling me all about that," said Nancy.

"Dr. Thompson, what's that car out on the track?" asked Indy.

"Oh, we're doing a little aerodynamic test. We'll be applying the information to our research on the automotive use of the electric battery," replied Dr. Thompson. "Now, if you'll give me that generator, I'll take it in to my assistant. I'm sure that he can have it ready for you by Saturday."

"Thank you!" said Nancy.

"I'll be back in a minute. Wait right here," said Dr. Thompson.

The race car circled the track three more times. Indy watched its every twist and turn.

Indy was no scientific genius. But Jewel had taught him a thing or two about how cars go.

It starts out with the fuel pump. The fuel pump takes gasoline from the tank in the car and pumps it through a filter to the carburetor. In the carburetor, the gasoline is mixed with air, which makes it ready to burn. Spark plugs ignite the fuel mixture, which makes the pistons go up and down. The pistons are connected to the crankshaft. When the pistons go up and down, the crankshaft turns and the car moves.

Indy could only imagine how fast those pistons must be pumping in that race car. By the time the car eased to a stop, Indy was worn out just thinking about it.

The driver shut off the deafening engine, then jumped out of the car.

"Hey, mister!" called Indy, racing over to the driver. "How fast can this thing go?"

"Indy! *Look out!*" shouted Nancy.

A van came screeching through the court-yard. Indy, Nancy, and the race car driver leaped out of the way to safety.

Looking at the van, they could see Dr. Thompson pounding desperately on the rear window.

They could see him mouthing the words, "Help! Help me!"

He was still calling for help when a huge hulk of a man dragged him back from the window. He disappeared into the darkness of the van.

That was the last they saw of Dr. Thompson. In seconds, the van went careening around a corner and out of sight.

Chapter 5

"Let's go to the lab!" said Nancy. "We may find some clues. Those guys who took Dr. Thompson might be kidnappers! They probably want Mr. Edison to ransom him."

When they got inside, they could hardly believe their eyes.

"They don't call this the Chemistry Lab for nothing!" said Indy.

The room was enormous. Lining the walls on both sides were a dozen great, long tables. On each table were shelves stacked with marked bottles of chemicals.

"Indy, listen!" said Nancy.

From somewhere in the room there came a muffled voice. "Mmm-mmph! Mmm-mmph!"

Indy and Nancy followed the sound. Under a table at the center of the room, they found a bound and gagged man lying in a heap on the floor.

Indy quickly untied him. Blood started oozing from the man's mouth as soon as Indy took off the gag.

"Who are you? What happened?" Indy asked.

"My . . . my name is . . . Dickinson," said the man, trying to catch his breath. "I'm Dr. Thompson's assistant. They kidnapped Dr. Thompson! Do you hear me? They kidnapped him!"

Nancy disappeared for a moment. She came back from the oak icebox with a cool damp cloth.

"Here, let me help you. You've got quite a nasty bruise on your forehead," she said.

While Nancy was tending to Mr. Dickinson, Indy inspected the damage done to the lab.

Chairs were overturned. Bottles were broken. At the far end of the huge room, Indy saw a smashed filing cabinet.

"Hey, Nance!" he called. "There's a cabinet here that's completely empty. The kidnappers must have stolen whatever was inside!"

"Oh, no!" Dickinson moaned, and staggered to his feet. "Call Security. Hurry!"

Before long, the lab was swarming with police. Detective Frank Brady of the West Orange Police Department was in charge of the investigation. He was a big, burly man with a gruff manner. On his head he wore a tan fedora that looked as if it had been planted there permanently.

"How many of them were there?" Detective Brady asked Nancy.

"There must have been at least three men," said Nancy. "I saw two in the front of the van.

And there was one more in the back. He's the one who dragged Dr. Thompson away from the window."

"Did you get a look at their faces?" asked the detective.

"No," said Nancy. "It was too dark in the van to see the man in the back. And the two men in front had their hats pulled way down. But the driver was thin. I could tell that from his narrow shoulders."

"Anything else?" asked the detective.

"The van was a supply van," said Nancy. "It was dark green and pretty grubby."

"Thanks, kids. I think that covers everything. You can go home now. Give Officer Ryan your names and addresses. If your families have telephones, be sure to give him the numbers. We'll be in touch if we need you," said Detective Brady.

"Is that all?" asked Nancy, sounding disappointed.

"That's all for now," said the detective.

Nancy had to spell Stratemeyer two times for

the police officer. Her eyes were glued to Detective Brady. He walked off to talk with Dickinson.

As soon as they could, Nancy and Indy slipped off to the side to listen. There was no way they were leaving now. They needed to hear what had happened.

"Please tell us anything you can remember, Mr. Dickinson," said Detective Brady.

"Just before I was slugged, one of the men said something. I think he was speaking German," said Dickinson.

"German? I can speak quite a bit of German," said Detective Brady. "Can you remember anything that was said?"

"It sounded something like *'Schnell die Huhnchen.'* Or maybe it was *'Bauerchen,'*" said Dickinson. "I can't remember."

"I think you may be a little confused," said the detective. "What you just said was, 'Quick, the baby's burping.'"

"No, sir," interrupted Indy. "I think that means 'Quick, the chicken's burping!'"

"Hey, kid, I know my German," said the detective. "*Bauerchen* means 'baby's burp.'"

"And *Huhnchen,*" said Indy, "is—"

Detective Brady was clearly annoyed. He wasn't going to let some teenager give him German lessons. "Look, kids, you're all finished here. You can go now," he said.

"Okay," said Indy. "But . . . but . . ."

"But what, kid? Spit it out," said the detective.

"Um, can we have our generator back?" asked Indy. "We'll be in big trouble with Nancy's father if we don't return it."

"Sorry," said Detective Brady, shaking his head. "That generator is evidence. Once the case is solved, maybe . . ."

At that very moment the door opened. An impressively large, white-haired man walked into the room.

He had sharp gray eyes and bushy white eyebrows. He was wearing a three-piece brown suit and a crisp white shirt. A black bow tie was neatly tied around his collar.

The room became totally silent. Everyone

44

seemed to stand a little straighter. It was almost as if they were standing at attention.

"Nance, it's him. It's Edison!" whispered Indy.

"Shhh!" hissed Nancy.

Without saying a word, Mr. Thomas Alva Edison, probably the greatest inventor who ever lived, walked across the room.

He went straight to the cabinet that had been broken into. He peered inside, then came back and stood eye to eye with Dickinson. "What did they take?" he asked in almost a whisper.

"They took Dr. Thompson, sir! They kidnapped him!" replied Dickinson.

"I already know that. I mean what research did they take? What designs?" boomed Edison. "Will somebody answer me?"

"They stole the Naval Consulting Board research files," said Dickinson.

When the war in Europe had started, Edison had suggested that a research laboratory should be created. Its purpose was to help develop better weapons for the Allies. A group called the Naval Consulting Board was formed. It was made up of the best researchers in the country.

Edison took his job as chairman very seriously.

"Were all the files kept in that cabinet? Are they *all* gone?" asked Edison.

"Yes, Mr. Edison. All of them," said Dickinson. "Even the project files on the submarine and torpedo detection units were taken. And the battery designs, too."

Edison shook his head slowly from side to side. He spoke in a voice so quiet that everyone had to strain to hear it.

"Those files were top secret," Edison said. "They were for the defense of our country, should we enter the war. We'd better bring in Naval Intelligence. Also, call President Wilson. He must be told immediately."

With those words, Edison turned and walked out of the room.

"That's it, then," said Detective Brady. "You're all free to leave now."

When they got outside, Indy said to Nancy, "Whatever the kidnapper was saying was pretty weird. I tell you, *'Huhnchen'* means 'chicken' in German. Actually, it means 'little chicken.' And

Bauerchen means 'baby burps.' But *Bauer* also means 'farmer.'"

Nancy's face lit up. It was as if one of Mr. Edison's light bulbs had gone on inside her head.

"Indy!" she said. "Remember we were looking out the window of the train on the way here? We saw a large barn. Do you remember what was painted on it?"

"You mean Van Hoecht's Poultry?" asked Indy.

It was Indy's turn to light up.

"Oh, my gosh! Of course! *Huhnchen* is 'chicken.' *Bauer* is 'farmer.' Chicken farmer!" he cried. "Let's ride down there and—"

Before he could finish his sentence, Nancy was halfway to the gate.

"Nancy! Wait for me!" he called.

Indy jumped on his bicycle. He had to pedal hard if he wanted to catch her.

Nancy is the most beautiful girl in the world, thought Indy. That I know. And she could be the smartest. But once, just once, I wish she wouldn't be the fastest!

Chapter 6

Nancy and Indy were pedaling down the road to the chicken farm. They talked as they rode.

"After you graduate from high school, you'll go to Princeton, of course," said Nancy. "I'm not sure where I'll go. Maybe Radcliffe or Vassar. But maybe someplace closer, so I can come home for the big weekends.

"After we get our degrees, we'll get married.

First we'll have Henry Jones the third, then two years later Sally," Nancy continued. "You'll be teaching at the university . . ."

"There you go again," said Indy.

"What?" asked Nancy.

"Organizing my life. Bossing me around," said Indy.

"Don't call me bossy!" said Nancy.

"Suppose I don't go to Princeton?" said Indy.

"Your father will get you into Princeton," said Nancy.

"I might want to go to the University of Chicago. It sounds like a more exciting place than Princeton. And I won't have my father breathing down my neck. Anyhow, we've got to get through high school first," said Indy.

"And we've got to get through the Valentine Dance before that!" said Nancy.

The chicken farm was just a few yards ahead. They rode through the gate and up the unpaved road. There it was—the barn with VAN HOECHT'S POULTRY written in big white letters on the roof.

"I don't see a van anywhere," said Indy.

"But look," said Nancy. "There are tire tracks going inside the barn. And it looks as if they're fresh."

Indy and Nancy leaned their bikes up against the gate. Then they followed the tracks inside the barn. The tracks stopped a few feet past the door. Several rakes and shovels were propped up against the walls.

"They must have covered up the rest of the van's tracks," said Nancy.

She and Indy stood there for a minute, studying the barn. There were stalls lined up on either side. There was hay stacked up everywhere they turned.

"Bull's-eye!" cried Nancy. "Look at that!"

A black slab of metal was sticking out of a stack of hay at the far end of the barn. Nancy raced over. Indy was right behind her.

They pulled at the hay. Sure enough, the black metal was part of a fender—the fender of the grubby green van!

Nancy walked around the van looking for clues. First she lifted the mudflap.

"Look at this, Indy," said Nancy. Her hand touched something thick and gooey. She sniffed her blackened fingers. "This is crude oil," she said.

"You're right," said Indy. "Interesting. I wonder where that came from."

Indy climbed into the van to see if he could find anything more.

He stopped for a minute to watch Nancy as she circled around to the front of the van. She was completely involved in her search, as if nothing else mattered. Indy thought of the other girls he knew. Some of them were always thinking about how they looked. But not Nancy. She was too interested in other things. Indy thought Nancy was prettier than any of those girls.

"Indy, I found something! This could tell us where the oil came from," called Nancy.

Indy jumped out of the van and joined Nancy up front. She was pointing to a sticker that was partly scraped off the windshield.

"Have you got a pen?" asked Nancy.

Indy found one in his pocket. He handed it to Nancy. She copied the letters from the sticker onto her hand: IL CH RY.

"It doesn't make much sense, does it?" said Indy.

"Not now. We'll figure it out later. Let's keep looking for more clues," said Nancy.

Thump. Thump. Thump.

"Shh! There's someone here!" whispered Nancy. "Cover up the van. Quickly!"

"Let's ride back to West Orange and get the police," whispered Indy. "Okay, Nancy? Nancy?"

Indy looked all around and inside the van. Nancy was gone.

He crouched down and slipped from stall to stall through the barn in search of her. Halfway across, he stepped on one of the rakes that was propped against a wall.

"Yeowch!" he squealed.

Meantime, the handle of the rake had knocked against a shelf. The shelf was tipping. Before Indy could get out of the way, dozens of cans and jars and boxes tumbled down onto his head.

The avalanche made quite a racket. And several of the boxes broke open on Indy's head. He was completely covered with white powder.

"Ptooey!" said Indy, spitting flour out of his mouth. "Mmm," he said, getting a lick of sugar off his cheek.

Suddenly Nancy was standing in front of him. "Eek!" she cried. "You look like a ghost. Are you okay?"

"Sure. Just add a couple of eggs, and pop me in the oven," said Indy.

"Very funny," said Nancy.

Thump. Thump. Thump.

"Listen," said Indy. "The noise is coming from the attic."

"Whoever is up there must have heard us," said Nancy.

She crept toward the steps.

"We're not going up there," said Indy. "No way!"

If he had been alone, he would have been upstairs already. But he worried about Nancy. She was brave and capable, but she was still a girl. Indy felt responsible for her.

Nancy knew just what to say to get Indy moving.

"Just because we happen to be on a chicken farm, that doesn't mean you have to act like a chicken," she said.

"Is that so? Well, I'll show you. I'm going first," said Indy.

"No way," said Nancy. "Ladies first."

"Age before beauty," said Indy.

"Intelligence before age," said Nancy.

"Hey, where did that come from?" said Indy.

"I don't know. I just made it up. That's because I'm so intelligent," said Nancy, grinning.

"All I know is I'm going to be faster!" said Indy, racing past Nancy onto the stairs. He was halfway up when he saw a broken step ahead of him. He leaped over it, then turned back to warn Nancy.

"Broken step. Be care-fulllll!" said Indy. He came crashing down through the next step, which was broken too.

Nancy grabbed the banister and got out of the way.

"Are you all right?" she asked. She was staring down at Indy sitting on the barn floor.

"I'm okay," he said, getting up and brushing himself off.

"Good!" said Nancy. And she raced up what was left of the stairs.

Nancy didn't find much in the attic. There were a few stray shovels and buckets, and a large wooden bookcase along the far wall.

Thump. Thump. Thump.

Nancy followed the sound. Soon Indy, looking ragged, was at her side.

As they got closer and closer to the far wall, the thumping got louder and louder.

Thump! Thump! Thump!

"It's coming from behind the bookcase!" said Indy. He pushed aside a stack of books and pulled at the wooden shelves.

The bookcase came sliding away from the wall. On the other side, something crashed to the floor.

Nancy walked into a small room that was lit by a single bulb hanging from the ceiling.

"Dr. Thompson!" shouted Nancy. "Thank goodness we found you!"

Chapter 7

Dr. Thompson was sitting in an overturned chair. He was bound and gagged. The chair must have fallen when Indy moved the shelves.

Indy quickly lifted the chair and untied Dr. Thompson.

"What a relief! As soon as I heard noises down in the barn, I started banging my chair. I hoped someone would hear me," said Dr. Thompson.

"I guess your banging and the fall must have loosened the ropes," said Indy. "Whoever tied them wasn't a boy scout."

"Where did the kidnappers go?" asked Nancy.

"I don't know. All I know is that they left me here to die! I am so grateful you found me. You'd better call the police. Quickly! We don't have much time," said Dr. Thompson.

In a few minutes, Detective Brady and his officers were searching the barn.

"For some reason, I am not surprised to see you two," said the detective. "Why don't you tell me what happened here."

Nancy and Indy took turns telling him the story. It clearly annoyed Detective Brady that Indy's German had proved to be better than his.

"Okay, thanks. Now, Dr. Thompson, it's your turn," said the detective.

Dr. Thompson told them about the kidnapping at the lab.

"I was completely surprised. I was just taking care of helping these fine young people get their generator fixed. Suddenly these two German fellows burst into my laboratory brandishing guns. And I didn't doubt for a moment that they were ready to use them."

"Did they identify themselves?" asked Detective Brady.

"They spoke English with a heavy accent," said Thompson. "I couldn't catch every word they said to me. The gist of it was that they were on a mission for the glorious cause of the German kaiser. When they spoke with each other, they spoke German. I only caught their first names—Kurt and Herman."

"Good German names," said Detective Brady. "There's no question that they were a couple of German agents. Please continue, Dr. Thompson."

"As soon as we got here they made me identify the antisubmarine plans. They said they would kill me if I didn't!" said Thompson. "I was so frightened I couldn't think fast. I should have given them plans for something else. Maybe I could have fooled them. Maybe . . ."

"That's water over the dam, Doctor," said

Detective Brady. "I can't worry about what you didn't do. Foreign agents have top-secret plans. We have to get them back. Did they say anything that might indicate where they were headed?"

"Let's see. My German is terrible. But I did keep hearing them say the words *Flut* and *Ebbe*," said Dr. Thompson.

"High tide! Low tide!" shouted Indy.

"High tide? Low tide? It sounds like someone was going to pick them up," said Detective Brady.

"Maybe a German submarine," said Indy.

Detective Brady nodded in agreement.

"They didn't say anything that might indicate *where* they were going to be picked up, did they?" asked the detective.

"Nothing I can remember," said Dr. Thompson.

Brady turned to Indy and Nancy.

"Okay, kids. Thanks again. But from now on, keep out of trouble, you hear me? This business could get dangerous," warned the detective.

Indy and Nancy said good-bye regretfully, then went to get their bikes.

"Indy, do you think the United States is going to join the war?" asked Nancy.

"It's possible. Even though President Wilson wants to keep us out of the fight, Teddy Roosevelt is certainly pushing for it. He keeps trying to paint a picture of Woodrow Wilson as a sissy intellectual because he was the president of Princeton University before he went into politics. But we don't have to worry about that right now," said Indy.

"I'm glad we rescued Dr. Thompson," said Nancy.

"Me too. Now I just hope the police will give us back the generator. Maybe Dickinson can fix it and get us to the dance in the Bugatti!" said Indy.

As they boarded the train back to Princeton, Nancy had more important things on her mind than the Bugatti.

"I wonder where that van came from," she said. "I can't stop thinking about that oil on the mudflap. If only we could . . ."

"Don't worry about it," said Indy. "Detective Brady will figure it out. And, remember, he told us to keep out of trouble."

"Trouble?" said Nancy with an impish grin. "That's my middle name!"

Indy smiled to himself. He couldn't have said it better.

"Say, am I still invited to dinner at your house tonight?" asked Indy.

"Mother is counting on it," said Nancy. "She's making your favorite—roast beef with mashed potatoes and gravy."

"I'll be there!" said Indy.

When he got back to Princeton, he went home to shower and put on fresh clothes. Indy always enjoyed having dinner at the Stratemeyers' house. At home, his dad usually sat at the table with his nose buried in a book. They never talked much. But it was different at Nancy's house. Everyone talked all the time.

As soon as they sat down to supper, they started talking about the Edison mystery. Nancy's dad was really excited about it. It was just the kind of adventure the writer of the Tom Swift stories could sink his teeth into.

"Whatever those Germans took must be pretty important," said Mr. Stratemeyer.

"Well, we know it was important enough to tell the president," said Indy. "By the way, Mrs. Stratemeyer, dinner is delicious. You make the best potatoes and gravy!"

"Thank you, Indy," said Mrs. Stratemeyer, smiling. "Here, let me give you some more." She made a tower of potatoes on Indy's plate. Then she covered it with gravy.

"You said they took *two* sets of plans?" continued Mr. Stratemeyer.

"Yes," said Nancy. "They took the detection system for submarines and—"

"And designs for an electric car battery," said Indy.

"Let's not forget that they also kidnapped Dr. Thompson!" added Mrs. Stratemeyer.

"No," said Nancy's dad. "They only took Thompson to use as a hostage in case they were cornered while escaping."

Mr. Stratemeyer sat up a little taller in his chair. Indy could see he enjoyed playing detective.

"But why would they steal plans for a battery?" asked Nancy.

"Maybe they're building an electric submarine!" said Indy.

"Mmm. I don't think so. It sounds to me as if they took the battery plans by mistake," said Mr. Stratemeyer.

"I wonder where that supply van came from. It was covered with oil," said Nancy.

"Maybe it was stolen from where the Germans landed," said her dad.

"You mean where the submarine dropped them?" asked Indy.

"Possibly," said Mr. Stratemeyer.

"Father, you're right!" said Nancy. "If only we knew where that was. Maybe that's where they're going to be picked up."

Nancy glanced at Indy. A plan was starting to take shape in her head. Indy wondered what it was this time.

"Well, I must say I'm surprised this doesn't

happen more often to Mr. Edison," said Nancy's dad. "Wherever there is true genius, there waits the unscrupulous opportunist ready to reap the fruits of ardent labor."

Mrs. Stratemeyer got a pained look on her face. She could tell when her husband was going to start on a long, drawn-out lecture. Once he got started, it was almost impossible to stop him.

"That is very interesting, dear," she said. "I think you've talked to us about geniuses before."

"Ah, but not Mr. Thomas Alva Edison. Just look around this house," continued Mr. Stratemeyer. "Edison has given us so much. The phonograph, the dictating machine . . ."

"I think I'd better clear away some of these dishes," said Mrs. Stratemeyer.

" . . . the kinetoscope," said Mr. Stratemeyer.

"If you'll excuse me Father, I think I'll go help Mother," said Nancy.

" . . . the mimeograph machine," said her father.

"I think I'll dry the dishes, sir," said Indy.

"Why, Edison even invented the incandescent light bulb!" said Mr. Stratemeyer.

He was becoming more and more excited, even without an audience.

Edward Stratemeyer jumped up and blew out the candles on the table. Then he flicked the light switch on the wall behind him. Nothing happened. He flicked the switch up and down, up and down. Still nothing happened.

He began pounding the wall. Suddenly the light bulb popped. Mr. Stratemeyer was left standing alone in the dark room.

Indy is hard at work at Harper's Ice Cream Parlor.

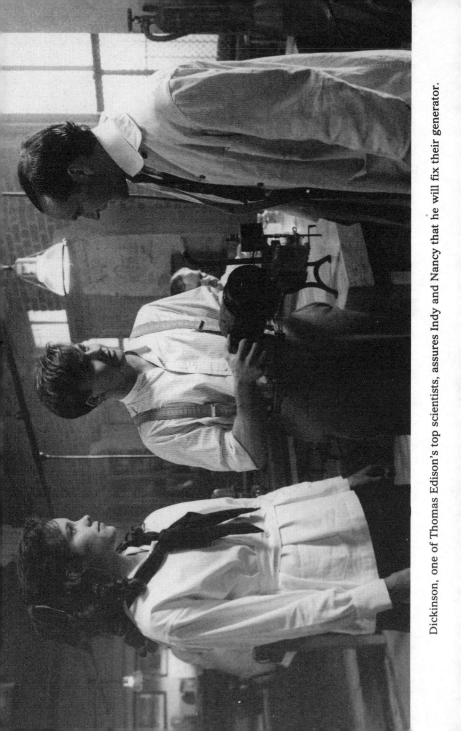

Dickinson, one of Thomas Edison's top scientists, assures Indy and Nancy that he will fix their generator.

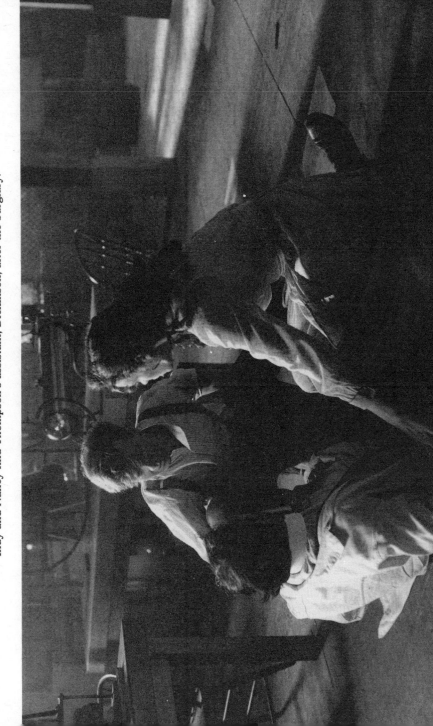

Indy and Nancy find Thompson's assistant, Dickinson, after the burglary.

Indy and Nancy describe the van they saw racing
from the laboratories to Detective Brady.

An angry Thomas Edison asks Dickinson which plans were stolen.

"Meet me after class," Indy writes in a note to Nancy.
"Meet *me* after class," his math teacher reprimands.

Nancy and Indy uncover the van used in the mysterious burglary.

Indy and Nancy search for clues in the dark basement of the oil refinery.

Indy and Nancy try to catch up to Dr. Thompson, who is speeding away in the race car.

After taking a shortcut, Indy's Model T actually *passes* Dr. Thompson in the race car.

Dr. Thompson realizes he is cornered.

Chapter 8

"Indy! Wait for me!" called Nancy at school the next day. She ran down the corridor to catch him.

"Hi. What's up?" asked Indy.

"Me. I was up all night thinking about things. It was like winding up a Victrola and playing the same song over and over again. But I've got it worked out now," said Nancy.

"You've got what worked out?" asked Indy.

"I know where the submarine is going to pick up the German spies. Remember the oil on the van's mudflap?" asked Nancy.

"Of course. You could hardly stop talking about it," said Indy.

"Well, that kind of oil could only have come from an oil refinery," explained Nancy. "And the only oil refineries near West Orange are in Bayonne. Bayonne is on the coast! Coast. Water. Submarines!"

"Did you tell the police yet?" asked Indy.

"Yes. But they wouldn't take me seriously," said Nancy. "I don't think the police pay attention to kids. Remember how Detective Brady gave you the brush-off when you tried to tell him that *Huhnchen* meant 'chicken'?"

"Well, you have to admit, the theory is a bit thin," said Indy.

"We've got to go there. I know I'm right. I just know it," said Nancy.

"Come on, Nancy. You want the two of us to take on a German submarine?" said Indy.

"Well, why not?" asked Nancy. "It's important."

"What's important to me right now is getting the generator fixed, getting to class, and then getting to work!" said Indy.

"Oh, come on, Indy. You know this is more important than any of that stuff. We've got to get those antisubmarine plans out of German hands. If we don't, thousands of people could die," said Nancy.

They stopped in front of their science room.

"Look, if you're right, we get ourselves killed. If you're wrong, I lose my job, and we lose the Bugatti!" said Indy.

"High tide today is at five P.M. I'm going to be there, whether you go with me or not," said Nancy.

She walked into the classroom, leaving Indy standing in the hall with his mouth hanging open.

By the last class of the day, Indy still had not decided if he should go. He could try one more time to talk Nancy out of going. But he knew from past experience that when Nancy made up her mind, there was no changing it.

Their math teacher was writing problems on the blackboard. Indy saw a note being passed from desk to desk to desk. It stopped in front of him. He opened it. It said ARE YOU COMING OR NOT?

It was now or never. He had to decide. Oh, who was he kidding? He had to go. There was no way he would let Nancy go alone. It was just too dangerous. He scrawled his answer on the paper and passed it back.

The note went from desk to desk to desk to . . .

"Jones!" called the teacher, grabbing the note. "You are supposed to be copying down math problems, not writing notes."

She opened the note and read it. It said MEET ME AFTER CLASS.

"Meet *me* after class, Mr. Jones," said his teacher.

Nancy looked exasperated. Butch, who liked nothing better than to see Indy get in trouble, was grinning from ear to ear.

Fortunately, Indy's after-school lesson on good behavior didn't take too long. Still, by the time he reached the bike shed, Nancy was already gone.

"She went that-a-way," said Ricky. "She said you'd know where she was."

"Thanks!" said Indy. He jumped on his bike and started pedaling.

"Hey, Clifford, take my shift at the soda shop, will you?" asked Indy.

"Whoa! The last time I did that, I almost put Mr. Harper out of business!" called Clifford.

"You can do it!" called Indy over his shoulder. "I know you can!" He pedaled away at breakneck speed.

When Indy got to the refineries at Bayonne, he rode across the sandy dunes toward the water.

A sign on a fence said in big letters: NO TRESPASSING. Of course, Nancy's bike was propped up right beneath it. Indy shook his head and grinned to himself.

Off in the distance, Indy saw someone moving across the dunes. It was Nancy. She had field glasses and a camera hanging around her neck.

"Nancy!" Indy called.

Nancy waved for him to come to where she was. She also motioned for him to keep quiet.

"Are you nuts?" said Indy when he reached her. "That sign said 'No Trespassing.' That means we are not supposed to be here."

"I know that. That's why we have to be quiet!" whispered Nancy.

"We could get shot!" answered Indy, trying to keep his voice low. "What if you had been gunned down before I got here? Alone. All alone. I can see the newspaper headlines now: GIRL MISSING FROM PRINCETON HOME—BODY FOUND ON BAYONNE BEACH."

"Stop worrying. As soon as we spot the submarine, we'll alert the coast guard station over there. I brought my camera, too, just in case. You never know," said Nancy.

"You mean so if one of us gets murdered, the other can take photos?" said Indy.

"Absolutely. I take the camera. You take the field glasses," said Nancy, handing them to Indy.

"Mr. Harper is probably planning his speech right now. You know—the long, sad one where he fires me for not showing up," said Indy. "I wonder how many glasses Clifford has broken and how many orders he got wrong."

"Oh, Indy. You know this is more important than serving up ice cream sundaes. If those plans get into German hands, thousands of people could die!" said Nancy. "Now come on."

"You're right," said Indy.

Indy followed Nancy up to another rise. They crawled on all fours until they reached a point where they could see down to the water. Indy looked through the field glasses.

"This is a good place," he said. "We can see them, but they can't see us."

"Okay. All we have to do is wait," said Nancy.

They were still waiting when the sun dropped out of sight and the sky turned blood red.

"It's now five forty-five," said Indy. "If they were coming at high tide like we thought, they would already have missed it."

"I don't understand this. Wait! Look!" whispered Nancy.

A car was driving out to the end of the jetty. Two men in trench coats were sitting inside. Nancy and Indy could not see their faces. But they could see that one of them was loading a gun.

"Get down!" said Indy, pushing Nancy down flat.

"Do you think they saw us?" asked Nancy.

She peeked up over the ridge.

"Run and get the coast guard. I'll wait here," said Indy.

"No, you go," said Nancy.

"I am not leaving you here alone!" said Indy.

"*DON'T MOVE!*" boomed a voice behind them.

Despite the warning, both Indy and Nancy swung around at the same time.

"Detective Brady! You *did* take me seriously," said Nancy, smiling.

"We've been here ever since you called us this morning, young lady," said the detective. "This business is too serious for us to ignore any tips."

"And nothing's happened?" asked Indy.

"Nothing until you two came along. Now it's time both of you went home. It's time we *all* went home," said the detective.

"Oh, brother," said Indy as he and Nancy left. "I missed work and lost my job for nothing. Well, you didn't want a corsage anyway, did you?"

"A corsage? What are you talking about?" said Nancy. "You know something, Indy. I wonder if Detective Brady was telling us the truth."

"Why wouldn't he?" asked Indy.

"Oh, I don't know. Anyway, I'm really sorry I dragged you out here," said Nancy.

"Forget it," said Indy.

They were just about to get on their bikes when Indy noticed oil tracks on the ground.

"Don't be too sorry. You were definitely right about where those oil tracks came from," said Indy.

Just then, the night lights of the refinery switched on, one after another. Soon the whole area was ablaze with light.

Indy looked off into the distance. All at once, he knew Nancy was right. Something important was going on.

Even if it meant losing his job, Indy was going to help figure out what it was.

Chapter 9

At one end of the long dining room table, Professor Jones was distractedly eating his dinner. He had a book called *The Canterbury Tales* propped open in front of him.

At the other end of the table, Indy was mindlessly pouring oil onto his salad. He was thinking about the events of his day. If he were having dinner at Nancy's house, he could talk about them. At the Stratemeyers' a family dinner was an occasion. At his house it was more like a study hall.

Indy was just plain uncomfortable with his father. And his stern, disapproving silence did little for Indy's appetite.

It had been different when his mother was around. Her soft, understanding presence cushioned his father's severity. He missed his mother very much, especially when he needed to share ideas.

Indy's mind was not on supper. He stared unseeingly at the steady stream of oil cascading down into his salad bowl.

Suddenly he shook his head as if waking from a dream. He put down the bottle and slammed his fist onto the table.

"Bless my dynamo!" cried Indy excitedly.

"Keep it down a little, Junior," said Professor Jones. He looked up from his book for an instant.

"I've got it! Father, may I be excused?" asked Indy.

Professor Jones had already gone back to his

book. Back to England in the Middle Ages. Hundreds of years and thousands of miles away from Princeton, New Jersey. Without looking up, he nodded to Indy to let him know he was excused.

Indy leaped from the table and raced to the telephone in the hall.

"Bless my dynamo?" muttered Professor Jones when Indy had gone. The Old English of *The Canterbury Tales* seemed less foreign to him than some of Indy's expressions.

"Hello, Mrs. Stratemeyer. It's Indy. May I please speak to Nancy?" he asked. Indy shuffled impatiently from one foot to the other. "It's important!"

Indy drummed his fingers on the table, waiting for Nancy to pick up the phone. Finally he heard her voice on the other end.

"Hi, Indy," said Nancy. "We were just finishing supper. Could you make it quick?"

"Nancy, we've got to go back to the refinery!" said Indy.

"It's really late, Indy. My parents will never let me out," said Nancy.

"But I figured out what's going on! The kidnappers weren't after the submarine plans. I'll bet you anything that they weren't German spies. They were from the oil company!" said Indy.

"Oh, my gosh! Are you sure?" asked Nancy.

"Sure I'm sure. They were after the electric car battery plans! They know that once the battery is perfected, they'll be put right out of business! It makes sense, doesn't it?" said Indy.

"That's right!" said Nancy. "The whole German business is probably just a hoax to fool everyone."

"So are you coming with me?" asked Indy.

For a moment there was silence on the other end.

"Hey, Nancy? Are you there?" asked Indy.

"All right, Indy. I'll help you with your homework. But this is the last time," said Nancy. Her voice was stern. She was obviously speaking for her parents' benefit.

"Great," said Indy. "I'll meet you at the train station in half an hour."

Indy wheeled his bike out of the old carriage house that served as a garage and stable. He carefully closed the latched doors behind him. Hopping on his bike, he steered down the tree-lined lanes and turned onto Nassau Street. The street was pretty quiet, considering it was the main street in town. There were hardly any university students in sight. Indy made good time. He pedaled past the neatly shuttered shops, remnants of colonial times. He coasted quickly past the two old hotels and the stately brick-and-stone bank. He turned right onto Railroad Avenue.

He thought for sure he'd have to wait for Nancy. But he didn't. She was already there, waiting for him with two round-trip tickets in her hand. They boarded the train to Bayonne.

"Now we know why they kidnapped Dr. Thompson. They wanted everyone to believe it was German spies at work," said Indy.

"With all the war talk going on, it seemed to make sense that there was a German plot. All along I thought there was something fishy about that," said Nancy. "But how are we going to prove it, Indy?"

"There's only one way. We've got to sneak in there and find those plans," Indy replied.

"Next stop, Bayonne!" called the train conductor.

Indy and Nancy carried their bikes off the train. Then they rode through the night without speaking. The sparkling lights of the refinery served as their guide.

They propped their bicycles up against a fence underneath a sign that said NEW JERSEY FUEL AND OIL.

"Indy!" said Nancy, holding out her hand.

"Nance, are you feeling a little scared? I'll hold your hand. You're the bravest girl in the world," said Indy.

"I don't want you to hold my hand, Indy. I just want you to look at it. Look at the letters. There are the letters I copied from the sticker on the van," said Nancy. "You can still read them."

"I-L . . . C-H . . . R-Y," read Indy. "Ilchry? Do we know what that means?"

"We do now! The first two letters on the sticker, *I* and *L*, were in the exact same type-face as on this sign. All that was missing was the *O*!" said Nancy.

"*O-I-L*. Oil!" cried Indy. "The van came from New Jersey Fuel and Oil."

"But we still have *C-H* and *R-Y*," said Nancy, reading from her hand. "What could those letters mean?"

"Let's go in and find out," said Indy, leading the way.

They walked along the pebbly gravel outside the gate. They stopped when they were a few feet from the security shed.

"We can wait here. When someone comes in or goes out, we'll try to slip by," whispered Indy.

Nancy nodded in agreement.

They did not have to wait very long. A car stopped in front of the gate on its way out.

The security guard opened the gate. Then he leaned down into the car window.

"How are you doing tonight, Mr. Hender-son?" asked the security guard.

"Not too bad, thanks," replied the driver.

"How's your wife feeling? I heard she wasn't well."

While the two men were talking, Indy and Nancy hunched down and hurried inside.

"Well, good night now," said the guard, closing the gate as the car drove through.

Before turning back to the shed, the guard caught sight of a shadow. He reached for his gun. Then he followed the shadows on their path to the refinery.

Chapter 10

Indy grabbed Nancy's hand, and they ran toward the hulking shapes of the refinery. The light cast an eerie glow. It was enough to show them outlines, but not enough to allow them to see clearly. They passed a storage tank, then disappeared into the first building they came to.

They had no idea where they were. It was

completely dark inside. They could hear some steamy, hissing sounds, and water dripping from overhead. They knew they must be in some kind of boiler room.

Suddenly a flashlight beam stabbed the darkness behind them.

"Come on!" whispered Indy. "The security guard must be checking up on us."

They weaved in and out between boilers and pipes. Indy did not let go of Nancy's hand for a minute. He was about to pull her down one more corridor when she pulled him back.

"Indy, look!" she said in a hushed voice. She pointed to a sign on a door:

RESEARCH LABORATORY

ONE FLIGHT DOWN

Nancy held out her hand and pointed to the letters: *CH . . . RY*.

At first Indy was puzzled. Then he looked back at the sign and nodded.

CH were the last letters in RESEARCH. RY were

the last letters in LABORATORY. The mystery of the sticker on the van was completely solved!

Indy pulled Nancy through a door leading to a stairway. Just a few seconds later the security guard's light fell on the spot where they had been standing.

Indy took his own flashlight out of his jacket pocket and led the way down the steep flight of steps.

"We should start a detective agency," whispered Nancy. "We could call it 'Jones and Stratemeyer.' Or maybe 'Nancy Jones, Super Sleuth.' Sounds good, doesn't it?"

"Nancy Jones, huh? I don't know," answered Indy.

"Shh!" whispered Nancy. "I hear noises coming from—"

All at once, the space below them was flooded with light. Their shadows were cast in giant relief against the wall behind them. Nancy and Indy dropped down flat on the steps. Nancy was on one step. Indy was right below her.

They listened to footsteps crossing the basement. Then, as quickly as the light went on, it was turned off again.

Indy cautiously led the way down to the landing. They tiptoed along the corridor until they came to a door marked RESEARCH LABORATORY.

From the crack at the bottom of the door, they could see that the light inside the room was on. As they got closer they could hear several voices inside. But the voices were too muffled for Nancy and Indy to make out the words. One thing was certain: Whatever the voices were saying, they weren't speaking German.

Nancy and Indy crouched down against the corridor wall. They held their breath and waited in total silence.

When the door opened, they could see three pairs of feet leaving the room. Nancy couldn't help noticing one shiny pair of two-toned shoes. Tan and black. She made a mental note. The other pairs were plain brown and black.

"This plan had better work," said one voice. "Edison's electric light bulb has all but destroyed the gaslight companies. We don't want that happening to us."

"Yes, sir," said a second voice.

"Just make sure the battery stays as weak as possible," said the first voice.

When the coast was clear, Indy and Nancy went into the lab to investigate. Indy shined his flashlight around the room. There was the usual lab equipment: filing cabinets, supply shelves . . .

"Nancy, look! There it is!" cried Indy.

Inside a glass case, like a precious jewel on display, was the file marked EDISON RE-SEARCH—STORAGE BATTERY.

Nancy tried to open the case. It was locked.

"Easy peasy," she said.

She pulled a hairpin from her hair and started picking at the lock. It still would not open.

"Here, let me try," said Indy.

He carefully removed the hairpin from the lock. Then he counted, "One, two, three!" With a skillful whack, he smashed the glass with the side of his flashlight.

"Madam, your hairpin," he said, handing it back to Nancy.

"Why, thank you," said Nancy.

"May I offer you a top-secret file?" asked Indy, pointing to the case where the file sat.

"Don't mind if I do," replied Nancy.

She carefully reached in and grabbed the plans. Drawing her hand past the jagged glass, she handed the plans to Indy.

Indy gave Nancy a quick kiss. "Now we've got to fly, my super sleuth!"

They had just stepped out of the building when they heard footsteps heading in their direction.

"Hide!" whispered Indy.

They dipped into the shadow of a giant oil tank and held their breath. They watched as two men hurried into the building.

"We've got to find out what that crash was about," said a voice.

"Those are two of the men we saw leaving the building before," whispered Nancy. "I recognize their shoes—brown and black."

"We'd better get out of here!" said Indy.

They ran through the refinery as fast as their legs would carry them. They were almost at the gate when they saw a car drive through. "I'll bet that's the man with the two-toned shoes. I wish I could see his face," said Nancy.

The security guard called, "Good night, sir!" Then he bolted the gate and disappeared inside his shed.

"Now what?" asked Nancy. "How the dickens are we going to get out of this place?"

Indy looked around. "I've got an idea," he said.

He led Nancy toward a truck loaded with massive oil barrels. The barrels were held in place by a wooden wedge. The truck was parked near a storage tank.

"It's worth a try," mumbled Indy.

"What is?" asked Nancy.

"Just stay with me and keep down!" said Indy.

He handed her the files. Then he picked up three rocks and threw them one by one to the top of the storage tank.

Sure enough, the security guard heard the noise and came to investigate.

"Get ready to run!" said Indy.

He picked up one last rock and hammered away at the wedge until the huge barrels came loose. They tumbled off the back of the truck, rolling toward the locked gates with enormous force.

As soon as they hit it, the gate was torn from its hinges.

"Now!" cried Indy.

Indy and Nancy made a mad dash through the gate.

"Stop!" shouted the guard. "Stop, or I'll shoot!"

Indy and Nancy kept running. The guard fired one warning shot into the air. Then he started to shoot directly at the retreating figures.

Chapter 11

Indy and Nancy hopped on their bikes and pedaled away from the refinery as fast as they could go. They thought they were only escaping the security guard's bullets. But the guard was not the only one after them.

Just as they were about to slow down, they heard car wheels screeching around the bend behind them.

Nancy couldn't make out the faces in the dark, but she recognized the car. It had been parked in the refinery. It had to belong to one of the two men who had gone back into the building.

"They're after us! Hurry!" cried Nancy.

"The road splits up ahead," said Indy. "Keep to the side of the road. I'll go left and divert them. You go right and get the police!"

"Done!" said Nancy. She turned her bike and went right.

Indy made sure he drew attention by taking the middle of the road. Then he went left. The car was soon following him, just as he had hoped.

Indy rode along the path until it met up again with the main road. When he reached the intersection, he saw the car closing in on him.

"Uh-oh!" cried Indy.

Fortunately he saw a path just ahead. Indy knew he had to take it, no matter where it would lead him.

The path was lined with thorny bushes on both sides. Indy had to pedal for all he was worth as the thorns ripped through his clothes and skin.

As he came up out of the path and back onto the road, his bike dipped into a deep pothole. He swerved back and forth. He swung both legs out, trying to keep his balance.

"We got him now!" called the driver.

Indy saw one more turn in the road up ahead. He hoped it would lead him to safety. But it wasn't a road at all. It was a pier.

"Look, he's not stopping!" called the man in the passenger seat.

"I have news for you," replied the driver. "We're not stopping either! We can't!"

Indy pedaled off the pier and went flying into the night sky. On the way down, he did a double somersault. Then he made a perfect jackknife dive down into the bay.

The car followed him into the water, making an enormous splash. For a moment there were no signs of life in the water.

Then Indy came bursting up through the ice-cold water. He looked around. There was no sign of the car. Seconds later, the two men struggled up to the surface, gasping for air.

Indy had nothing to fear. Nancy and Detective Brady were waiting on the pier.

"Indy! Indy, are you all right?" called Nancy.

"Sure!" called Indy as he climbed out of the water. "Did you catch that dive I did?"

"Too bad I didn't snap a picture," said Nancy. She wrapped a blanket that had been in the police car around him.

Meanwhile, the police dragged the two men from the bay and carted them off in their police vans.

"Well done, kids," said Detective Brady. "I never would have guessed the oil company was behind all this. You're good detectives. I'll bet you get a big reward for this."

"Oh, we don't want a reward," said Nancy.

"No, we'd just like to be the ones to take those files back to Dr. Thompson," said Indy. He pointed to the files that were now in Detective Brady's hands.

"Sure, why not?" said the detective.

He handed the files to Indy.

Indy and Nancy made plans to deliver the files to the Edison laboratory the next day. When they arrived at the plant, they found Dr. Thompson hunched over his desk in the Chemistry Laboratory. Ever since the electric battery plans had been stolen, he had been working on one thing—recreating them.

"Good morning, Dr. Thompson! Guess what?" said Nancy brightly. "We did it! We really did it!"

Dr. Thompson looked up from his work. He looked pale and tired. The last thing he wanted was a couple of teenage visitors.

"Did what?" he asked.

"We found the battery plans!" said Indy.

"What are you talking about?" asked Dr. Thompson. "Is this some sort of a prank?"

"It's no prank, sir. Look!" said Indy.

He presented the folder containing the secret plans to Dr. Thompson.

"But—but how did you do it?" stammered Dr. Thompson.

"They tried to fool you with that German spy routine. I must say it almost worked," said Indy.

"It certainly fooled Detective Brady and the police."

Thompson leafed through the file.

"I hope everything is there," said Nancy.

"Yes, yes, everything. I can hardly believe it. It's incredible. Well done!" said Dr. Thompson.

"I remembered what my father said to you at dinner the other night. He said that this new electric battery would put the oil companies out of business. That gave us the motive. Then Nancy found crude oil on the van. One thing led to another and . . ."

"You mean you stole these back from the refinery?" asked Dr. Thompson.

"That's right, sir," said Indy.

"But how did you know where to go?" asked Dr. Thompson.

A sudden shiver went up and down Nancy's spine. She tried to signal Indy without letting on that anything was wrong. But he was too excited to notice.

"Like I told you, Nancy found crude oil on the van. At first we connected it to the Germans. Then when nothing on that end panned out, we started thinking about the refinery. And then there was the motive, staring us right in the face," said Indy.

"Yes, well, I'd better put these in the safe," said Dr. Thompson.

"Indy," whispered Nancy when Dr. Thompson was out of earshot. "How did he know about the *refinery*?"

"What?" mouthed Indy.

"We didn't tell him we were at the refinery. So how did he know?" asked Nancy.

Dr. Thompson was struggling with the lock on the cabinet at the far end of the laboratory. Even from a distance Nancy could not help noticing his shoes. They were two-toned. Tan and black.

"It was Dr. Thompson all along! He's the one who stole the plans," whispered Nancy.

"Dr. Thompson?" asked Indy.

"The shoes! Look at his shoes!" whispered Nancy. "He set it up. The kidnapping. The fake German spies. Everything! Remember how easy it was to untie him?"

"Let's go," said Indy, leading the way across

the lab. "Dr. Thompson owes us a few answers."

Dickinson had been listening to Nancy and Indy the whole time. He stopped what he was doing and followed at a safe distance.

"Why, Dr. Thompson?" asked Indy.

"Why what?" said Thompson, spinning around to face him.

"Why did you steal your own plans?" asked Indy.

"You were at the refinery last night, weren't you?" said Nancy.

Dr. Thompson glared at Nancy and Indy.

"Why, why, you . . ." he hissed. "You busybodies think you can undo a lifetime of work. Ruin a man's whole career!"

"Dr. Thompson, I think you'd better hand those plans back to us," said Indy.

"You meddling little brats!" Thompson shouted. "Why couldn't you mind your own business!"

"Give back the plans!" repeated Indy.

Thompson looked around like a cornered animal. There was no way out on the far side of the lab. He pushed Indy and Nancy out of his way and ran.

Indy grabbed his arm and swung him around. Dr. Thompson took a fistful of Indy's hair and smashed Indy headfirst into a wall.

"You can't get away with that!" cried Nancy. She leaped onto Thompson's back and hung on with all her might. Thompson was spinning round and round. Then Nancy lost her grip and went flying into a wall of glass tubes. A burst of chemicals and shattered glass cascaded through the air.

"Nancy! Are you all right?" called Indy, staggering to her side.

Dickinson raced back from the lab safety station with a fire ax. He waved it threateningly in Thompson's direction.

"Stand still, Dr. Thompson," said Dickinson. "I don't want to use this. Please don't make it necessary."

Thompson grabbed a bottle that was labeled ACID. He smashed it to the ground and ran!

Poisonous fumes filled the air.

"Cover your faces and run for it!" shouted Dickinson to Indy and Nancy.

They raced out of the lab in time to see Thompson disappear into the shed. A moment later he came speeding out in the race car.

"I'm calling the police!" cried Dickinson. "He has no right to take that car! It's company property!"

"We can't let him get away!" cried Indy.

He spotted a Model T parked outside the building.

"Let's go!" said Indy.

"Whose car is it?" asked Nancy.

"Who cares? Just get in!" said Indy.

Indy cranked up the car and hopped into the driver's seat. Nancy was already next to him. Then they took off—as fast as a Model T could go.

Chapter 12

Luckily, Dr. Thompson had been held up at the gate. Someone in front of him was asking the security guard for directions. Indy reached the gate just as the security guard was closing it.

He swerved and drove around and out another gate. He got to the street in time to see Dr. Thompson turning a corner.

The streets were narrow, and Thompson knew them well. That was one big advantage. The second—and greater—advantage was that he was driving a race car. Meanwhile, Indy and Nancy were stuck in a Model T.

"Hurry, Indy! Don't let him get away!" said Nancy.

"This thing can't go any faster," said Indy.

Thompson zoomed down the street. People were flying every which way, trying to avoid being hit by the two cars.

"Watch out!" cried Nancy.

Indy swerved around an old woman who had stepped out of nowhere into his path.

When he was back on course, he saw Thompson turning left. Indy turned left and found himself on a dirt road. They watched Thompson's car grow smaller and smaller as it got farther and farther ahead of them.

"What are we going to do?" said Nancy.

"There's a fork in the road up ahead. It might be a shortcut. We'll just go left there," said Indy. "It's our best bet, Nance."

When Thompson looked behind him, all he

saw was an empty road. He smiled to himself and kept on going.

"Uh-oh, Indy! We're not going to make it!" cried Nancy.

A sign in the center of the road said STOP! BRIDGE OUT.

"We can do it," said Indy. "Hold on!"

Nancy grabbed the wheel.

"When I said hold on, I didn't mean hold on to the wheel! Let go of it! Let go!" cried Indy.

"No. We can't make it!" said Nancy.

"Oh, yes, we can!" said Indy.

He smashed through the barrier and bumped over the broken-down bridge. Wooden slats were falling into the water. It felt like the bridge was coming apart all around them.

But, miracle of miracles, they made it across.

"Hey, how about that?" said Indy. "Even *I* thought it would collapse."

"Great," said Nancy. She breathed a sigh of relief now that they were again on firm ground.

The dirt road led them back onto the highway.

"If we just keep going," said Indy, "we're bound to catch—"

"I see him!" called Nancy. "Slow down."

"Why?" asked Indy.

"Because you just passed him," said Nancy.

"I told you that road we took was going to be a shortcut!" said Indy.

Just then Thompson pulled alongside the Model T. He looked over and saw Indy and Nancy. Then he swerved to the right and rammed them hard.

"Get him," called Nancy.

Indy rammed Thompson right back.

Thompson hit Indy again, harder than before. The wheels of the two cars locked.

Thompson dragged the Model T down the highway a hundred feet. At last the two linked cars came apart with a clanking thud.

Both of the cars were speeding down the narrow highway. When the cars rounded a curve, a truck was heading their way. But it wasn't just a farm truck. No, it wasn't heaped high with bags of seed. No, it wasn't carrying eggs to market or milk to a bottling plant.

Its cargo was as dangerous as death on wheels.

"Do you see what I see, Indy?" said Nancy, bracing herself.

"You mean the truck that says 'Acme Dynamite'?" said Indy.

"Yup," said Nancy. "I'd say it was heading our way, wouldn't you?"

"Yup," said Indy. "He's heading right for us! Hold tight, Nance. And, just in case, it's been great knowing you!"

The truck driver's eyes opened wide with fear. He slammed on his brakes and skidded to a stop just before the road branched off.

Thompson drove left. Indy drove right. Then Indy quickly doubled back to follow Thompson.

As they were passing the dynamite truck, Nancy and Indy heard a deafening *pop!* They were sure they were all about to become history.

But as they whizzed past they could see the

truck was still standing upright. The only thing wrong with it was a blown-out tire—and a totally stunned driver.

"I don't see any sign of Thompson," said Nancy. "Where do you suppose he went, Indy?"

They kept on driving until they came to a dead end. Indy turned the car around and started back. In the distance they could hear the wail of police car sirens.

"Look! There are tire tracks going through that puddle," said Nancy.

Indy took a sharp right and stepped on the gas hard. Suddenly he found himself facing Thompson's car head-on. They were on a collision course!

Thompson swerved up into a field.

Indy swerved down into the embankment. The car tipped over on its side, and Indy went flying into Nancy.

"Are you okay, Nancy?" asked Indy.

"Uh-huh. How about you?" asked Nancy.

"I'm all right," said Indy. "Let's get out of here."

They climbed up out of the car, which took a

bit of doing. Then they climbed up the slippery embankment and looked around. Detective Brady was leading Thompson to the police car across the field.

"Dr. Thompson, why did you do it?" asked Nancy.

"Every man has his price," said Thompson bitterly.

"You did it for money?" asked Indy.

"Stealing those plans would not have stopped the electric car from coming. The only difference was, I would have the money to start my own company. My *own* company. Do you understand what that means to me?" said Thompson. "Do you understand what it's like to have another man get credit for your work?"

"Let's go," said Detective Brady impatiently.

"I wanted what was mine! I did all the work!" shouted Thompson.

Then the door to the police car shut, and Thompson disappeared.

Indy and Nancy drove back to the Edison laboratories to return the car and look in on Dickinson.

When they walked into the Chemistry Lab, Mr. Edison was there, leafing through the plans. With the plans back in his hands, Mr. Edison seemed like a new man. He was beaming with delight.

"Miss Stratemeyer! Mr. Jones! Thank you both for a job well done," said Edison happily. "One day my new battery will make the electric car a truly practical alternative."

"I hope so," said Nancy.

"The whole world will thank the two of you! You must come and test drive the car when it is finished," continued Mr. Edison.

"Wild horses wouldn't keep us away, sir!" said Indy.

"I wish we had that car for you now," said Dickinson. "Your generator isn't going to do you much good."

Dickinson handed the Bugatti generator to Indy.

"Oh, I understand. There wasn't time to fix it with everything that's happened," said Indy. He couldn't quite hide his disappointment.

"I'm sorry," said Dickinson.

"Oh, well, Nance. I guess we'll have to ride with Ricky after all," said Indy.

But Mr. Edison had another solution in mind. He smiled as he told Indy and Nancy what it was.

On the night of the dance, Butch and Rosie drove up in Butch's shining Model T. They made quite a stir as they stepped out of the car, dressed like movie stars.

"Whoa!" said Clifford. "Look at these two. They're the cat's pajamas!"

Butch checked his reflection in the shiny hood of his Model T.

"Anybody see the soda *jerk* yet?" he asked. "Is he out back tying up his horse? Or was he too ashamed to show?"

Butch was interrupted by the roar of a motor.

"Oooh!" said Rosie. "If wishes were horses! Look at that car!"

Indy and Nancy pulled up to the school in Mr. Edison's gleaming race car.

"Whoa! Allow me!" said Ricky. He ran to open the door.

When Nancy stepped out, in her pink lace dress with a matching pink-and-white corsage, everyone gasped. They lined up on either side of the entrance to the dance. Even Butch and Rosie stepped back to let Indy and Nancy pass.

Indy took Nancy's arm and led her up the stairs.

Before they went in, he turned to her and whispered, "You are the greatest, Nancy Stratemeyer. You've got brains, luck, and dollops of pluck!"

"Dollops of pluck?" said Nancy. "Is that a compliment?"

"You bet," said Indy.

Then they went inside and danced until dawn.

Historical Note

Thomas Edison never did finish his work on the electric battery for the car. The majority of automobiles continue to be fueled by gasoline. And gasoline companies continue to thrive.

Cars have, of course, come a long way since they were invented. The first compact "internal-combustion" engine was built in 1862 by a Frenchman named Jean Joseph Étienne

Lenoir. He mounted his engine between the wheels of an old horsecar. His engine worked by burning gas inside a cylinder. Amid the horse-drawn carriages, this first "car" chugged along the streets of Paris.

Soon engines were made to run on gasoline. In 1885, a manufacturer in Germany, Karl Benz, began selling cars to the public. These cars were able to go up to 20 mph. But they were not very reliable. So people often traveled with their horses trotting along behind them in case of trouble.

The first cars were thought to be such a strange creation that they were shown in circuses. But it didn't take long for people to make cars part of their lives.

By the 1920s, cars could travel more than 100 mph. Sports cars were sold for the fun of fast driving. Some of the best sports cars were made by Alfa Romeo, Bentley, Chevrolet, Duesenberg, and of course, Bugatti—like Edward Stratemeyer's car.

Today, about 340 million passenger cars travel on highways around the world. People use their cars to get to and from work, and to travel for pleasure.

But with this widespread use of gasoline-powered cars comes exhaust. This poisonous exhaust is responsible for one of the most pressing problems facing our planet today: air pollution.

Cars in the United States use about 121 billion gallons of gasoline a year. This need for gasoline leaves us at the mercy of certain Arab nations that produce it. In 1973, these nations stopped shipping gasoline to the United States for five months for political reasons. Gasoline prices soared, and it took hours of waiting in line to get the chance to fill up a tank at the service station because of the gas shortage.

These problems would become less pressing if there were a reliable electric car. The power in an electric car comes from one or more electric motors. The motors are run on rechargeable batteries.

Since there is no gasoline used, there is no exhaust and no dependency on foreign suppliers. Electric cars are quiet. And they can be recharged at home, instead of at a service station.

Electric cars do exist. The first ones appeared in Europe in the 1880s. By the late 1880s, Americans drove more electric cars than gasoline-powered cars. But by the early 1900s, gasoline-powered cars proved to be more powerful and cheaper to operate. By the late 1920s, electric cars had all but disappeared from everyday use.

New interest in electric cars came in the 1960s as our concerns about pollution grew. In the 1970s production of electric cars began again on a limited basis. But few electric cars are sold today because they are expensive and still do not perform as well as gasoline-powered cars. Electric cars do not travel as fast, and the batteries need to be recharged at least every 100 miles.

Manufacturers are trying to create better batteries for electric cars, so that the cars will go faster and will not need to be recharged so frequently.

Imagine if Thomas Edison were alive today.

One of his greatest gifts was that he used his scientific genius to improve the quality of everyday life. Edison was said to be quite a tyrant. His New Jersey laboratory did not always run smoothly. But it was still the beginning of the modern research laboratory in which teams of workers, rather than a lone inventor, worked together to solve a problem.

People are working today to develop a practical electric car. We may all have the chance to drive one before too long.

TO FIND OUT MORE . . .

The Story of Thomas Alva Edison by Margaret Cousins. Published by Random House, 1965, paperback, 1980. Tells the life story of one of the most influential inventors of all time. Describes how Edison viewed the electric car and why his version failed. Drawings and photos.

The Roads We Traveled: An Amusing History of the Automobile by Douglas Waitley. Published by Julian Messner, 1979. Traces the history of the automobile. Includes the blunders and failures as well as the triumphs. The history of the electric car is discussed. Photos and bibliography.

Antique Cars by Robert B. Jackson. Published by Henry Z. Walck, 1975. Descriptions of fourteen antique cars tell the story of the automobile's first forty years. The Ford Model T, Oldsmobile, Buick, and Packard are among the cars featured. Lists the names and locations of antique car museums throughout the U.S. and Canada. Photos.

Electric Cars by E. John DeWaard & Aaron E. Klein. Published by Doubleday, 1977. Describes the rise and fall of the electric car through the twentieth century—how it worked and why, to date, it has failed. Discusses how electric cars can be an alternative to gas guzzlers. Photos.

Inventions No One Mentions by Chip Lovitt. Published by Scholastic, 1987. Edison's electric car was not as successful as he had hoped, and the same goes for the inventions in this book. The hair-growing hat, the air-conditioned rocking chair, the mechanical snowball thrower, and eye protection for chickens are some of the hilarious inventions that didn't survive. Photos and drawings.

Why Didn't I Think of That: From Alarm Clocks to Zippers by Webb Garrison. Published by Prentice-Hall, 1977. We know Thomas Alva Edison invented the light bulb, but who invented the ballpoint pen? What about the elevator, blue jeans, safety pin, or telephone directory? Find out in this book that describes the origin of everyday objects we now take for granted. Illustrations.